Stephen Gammell

Once Upon MacDonald's Farm...

Four Winds Press
New York

LIBRARY OF CONGRESS CATALOGING IN
PUBLICATION DATA   GAMMELL, STEPHEN.
    1. Once upon MacDonald's farm.
Summary: MacDonald tries farming with circus
animals, but has better luck with his neighbor's
cow, horse, and chicken.
(1. Farm life – Fiction. 2. Animals – Fiction)
I. Title.
PZ7. G1440n (E)   80-23956
ISBN 0-590-07792-9

Published by Four Winds Press
A division of Scholastic Inc. New York, N.Y.
Copyright © 1981 by Stephen Gammell
Printed in the United States of America
Library of Congress Catalog Card Number: 80-23956
    1 2 3 4 5 85 84 83 82 81

To my dear One,
my family
and Sully...

While it is true that MacDonald had a farm...

it wasn't much of a farm,

and he had *no* animals.
None at all.

So, he bought an elephant...

he also bought a baboon and a lion.

In the morning, MacDonald and the elephant went out to the field...

to do the plowing.

Much later that afternoon,

there were still some chores
to be done.

Eggs to gather...

Milking to do...

MacDonald was weary, and went to bed early.

But while he slept, the animals decided to leave. And did...

without a sound.

When MacDonald awoke, he had no animals...

but his neighbor offered
to help.

That evening, he sent over
a horse, a cow and a chicken.

MacDonald was thankful for
his new animals.

So, after a good sleep and a healthy breakfast, he was eager to start work.

He had eggs to gather, the milking to do...

But first the plowing.